APR 2 5 2017

For Dad x
~ P. B.

For Amanda, Hilary, Lydia, Mary, Thérèse, Vanessa,
and Yvo, who would love Bear's house of books!
~ A. E.

tiger tales
5 River Road, Suite 128, Wilton, CT 06897
Published in the United States 2017
Originally published in Great Britain 2017
by Little Tiger Press
Text by Poppy Bishop
Text copyright © 2017 Little Tiger Press
Illustrations copyright © 2017 Alison Edgson
ISBN-13: 978-1-68010-038-9
ISBN-10: 1-68010-038-6
Printed in China
LTP/1400/1650/0816

For more insight and activities, visit us at www.tigertalesbooks.com

BEAR's House of Books

by Poppy Bishop

Illustrated by Alison Edgson

tiger tales

Once there lived four friends who loved stories. Every night at bedtime, they read the same worn-out storybook. The cover was scuffed and the pages were sticky, but they didn't mind one bit. It had been theirs since they were all very little.

"Wouldn't it be nice," said Mouse one day at breakfast,
"to read a new book?"

"A new book?" cried Fox. "But where would we get one?"

"Maybe you dig them up like potatoes,"
said Hedgehog hopefully.

"I know!" cried Rabbit. "They fall from the sky like shooting stars!"

"Let's go on a book hunt and find out," said Mouse.

So they packed peanut butter and jelly sandwiches and set out on their adventure.

The friends searched the woods high and low.

"This is silly," grumbled Fox after a while. "You can't just *find* books."

"Then what's that?" said Hedgehog, pointing at something red under a bush. It had thick pages, a big black title, and smelled exactly like . . .

"A BOOK!" cheered Mouse. "It's a book!"

And what a fantastic story it was—
with a fire-breathing dragon for Rabbit,
and a happy ending for Hedgehog.
"That was magical," Hedgehog sighed.
"It's my new favorite story,"
declared Fox.

But Mouse saw something written inside.

KEEP YOUR PAWS OFF!

The Other Side of the Woods
Thorny Lane
The Twisted Oak
Bear
This book belongs to:

"Oh, no!" said Hedgehog. "We had better return the book right away."

"Can't we keep it a little longer?" asked Rabbit.

But deep down, the friends knew that they shouldn't.

This book belongs to:
Bear
the Twisted Oak
Thorny Lane
the other side of the Woods
KEEP YOUR PAWS OFF!

It was a long, hot walk to Bear's house.
When they got there, no one answered Rabbit's
loud RAT-A-TAT-TAT on the door—and the
book wouldn't fit through the mailbox.

"Now what do we do?" huffed Fox.

"Look! An open window!" squeaked Mouse.

The friends lifted up
the heavy book to push it
through the window.

But Mouse forgot to
let go and fell in after it!

BUMP!

BUMP!

WHUMP!

"Ouch!" cried Mouse, landing
on a huge pile of . . .

. . . books! They were everywhere! Thin books, thick books. Funny books, sad books. Whole new worlds to hold in their hands.

"Look!" Mouse beamed as she let her friends in.

"Wow!" gasped Rabbit. "So many adventures!"

"And happy endings!" cheered Hedgehog.

"Let's start reading!" said Fox.

Many wonderful stories later, the friends heard a **THUMP!**

"What was that?" gasped Fox.

It was getting closer . . . **THUMP! THUMP!**

And louder! **THUMP! THUMP! THUMP!**

"Someone's coming!" whispered Rabbit.

"Oh, no!" cried Hedgehog. "This isn't our house, and these aren't our books!"

"Quick!" whispered Mouse.
"Hide!"

Bear clomped into the room. He sat down with a HUFF and reached for a book.

"Who left sticky pawprints on this cover?" he grumbled. "And a SANDWICH in the middle!" he rumbled.

"WHO'S BEEN READING MY BOOKS?!"

"We have," quavered four little voices.

"Who are you?" bellowed Bear, pulling back the curtain.

"And what are you doing here?"

"We're very sorry," squeaked Mouse.

"We found this book in the woods and—"

"That's mine!" cried Bear.

"It's my favorite!"

"It's our favorite, too," said Rabbit.

"I liked the end," Hedgehog whispered. "I love happy endings."

"HMMPH!" grumped Bear. "I like happy endings, too."

The four friends headed toward the door.

"We're really sorry," said Mouse. "We have only one book at home."

"Wait," frowned Bear. "Only one book?"

He thought for a moment, and then picked a storybook from the shelves. "If you wash your sticky paws, you can stay and read with me."

So Bear and the friends piled into an
armchair and read the story together.
They had so much fun that
they read another, and
another, until it was
time to go home.

"Can we come back?" asked Rabbit.
"Hmmph!" said Bear. Then he smiled.
"I'd like that very much."

So the friends came back the very next day. They even
read Bear their own worn-out storybook.
    And that gave Bear a very good idea . . .
because books are wonderful to read alone,
but even better when shared.

DATE DUE

DEMCO 128-8155